For my ocean-loving nieces and nephews,
Dylan, Adelaide, Adam, Marina, and Orion
—M. F.

For F. and our childhood
—P. Z.

BEACH LANE BOOKS
An imprint of Simon & Schuster Children's Publishing Division
1230 Avenue of the Americas, New York, New York 10020
Text copyright © 2020 by Meg Fleming
Illustrations copyright © 2020 by Paola Zakimi
BEACH LANE BOOKS is a trademark of Simon & Schuster, Inc.
For information about special discounts for bulk purchases, please contact
Simon & Schuster Special Sales at 1-866-506-1949 or business@simonandschuster.com.
The Simon & Schuster Speakers Bureau can bring authors to your live event. For more information or to book an event,
contact the Simon & Schuster Speakers Bureau at 1-866-248-3049 or visit our website at www.simonspeakers.com.
Book design by Rebecca Syracuse.
The text of this book is set in The Hand.
The illustrations are rendered digitally.
Manufactured in China
0220 SCP
First Edition
1 2 3 4 5 6 7 8 9 10
Library of Congress Cataloging-in-Publication Data
Names: Fleming, Meg, author. | Zakimi, Paola, illustrator.
Title: Here comes ocean / Meg Fleming ; illustrated by Paola Zakimi.
Description: First edition. | New York : Beach Lane Books, [2020] | Summary: Illustrations and simple,
rhyming text follow a child through a day of surprises at the beach.
Identifiers: LCCN 2019010178 | ISBN 9781534428836 (hardcover : alk. paper) | ISBN 9781534428843 (eBook)
Subjects: | CYAC: Stories in rhyme. | Beaches–Fiction. | Ocean–Fiction.
Classification: LCC PZ8.3.F639 Her 2020 | DDC [E]–dc23 LC record available at https://lccn.loc.gov/2019010178

HERE COMES
OCEAN

written by Meg Fleming ⭐ illustrated by Paola Zakimi

BEACH LANE BOOKS

NEW YORK   LONDON   TORONTO   SYDNEY   NEW DELHI

Sun beach. Rise beach. Pail in hand.
Found a dollar in the sand!

Cool those toes.
What next? Who knows?

Here
comes
ocean!

Soft beach. Warm beach. Dig a seat.
Something's nibbling on my feet.

Hide those toes.
What next? Who knows?

Here
comes
ocean!

Salt beach. Breeze beach. *Look, a track!*
Pipers chase the water back.

Sink those toes.
What next? Who knows?
Here comes ocean!

Low beach. Tide beach. Treasure store.
Ropy lassos line the shore.

Splash those toes.
What next? Who knows?

Here
comes
ocean!

Loud beach! Crash beach! Prickly walk.
Sea star clinging to a rock.

Plant those toes!
What next? Who knows?

Here comes ocean!

Oh, beach. No, beach! *Better run!*
Giant wave in 3... 2... 1!

Move those toes. What next?

Too
MUCH
ocean!

Slow beach. Down beach. Sky grows pale.
Stained-glass sailors. Purple trail.

Dry those toes.
What next? Who knows?
Here comes ocean.

Moon beach. Night beach. Sparkly swish.
Wish upon a night-light fish.

Snug those toes.
What next? *You* know.

Night-night, ocean.

SEAGULL

SHELL

CRAB

SANDPIPER FEATHER

SAND DOLLAR